The Adventures of
Charlie, Blue and
Larry Lamp Post

Sarah, Duchess of York

illustrated by Emma Stuart

ENDORSEMENT

I think this book is great!

I love how you chose the colours of Charlie's jumper (this is the colour of the Rabbitoh's rugby league team jersey).

I am glad you chose a good colour for Charlie's skin as well.

I love the story of the stars.

Pauline Deweerd
Executive Director – Aboriginal Health
St Vincent's Health Network, Sydney

DEDICATION

For everyone reading this book,
and for children please never give up
the curiosity of wanting to learn more.

Look up to the sky, let the stars guide you,
and learn about the wonderful
old cultures of love and traditions.

I honour first nation all over the world.
Thank you for being steadfast
to what you believe.

Sarah, Duchess of York

Before Blue came, Charlie was lonely. Mum had forgotten how to smile since she lost her job. Dad was hardly ever home. When he wasn't working at the observatory, he was helping homeless people find hope and shelter.

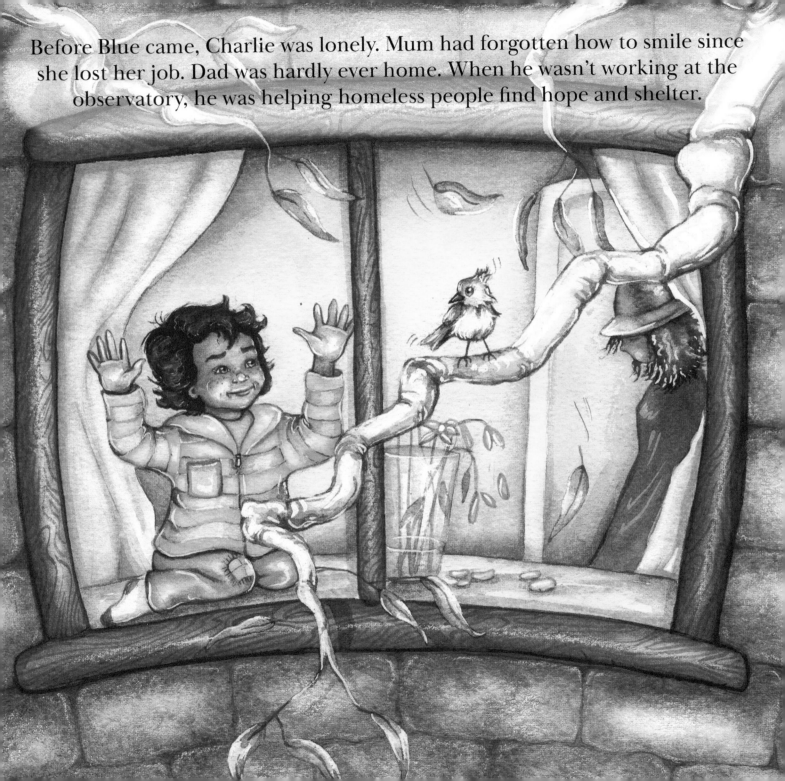

Dad was a man who had always wished he had travelled to the moon, through the stars and galaxies, and any time that Charlie could he would spend the day at the observatory.

Charlie tried his best to make his mum happy. He would find flowers tucked in tarmac and realise how strong and brave the flower must be to fight through and bloom. He looked at the flower stall and thought Mum would be happy if he returned with a new friend Billy Barrow who was filled with beautiful flowers.

He always managed to see hope and colour through the darkness and wondered if it was because of his love of stars and maybe a little stardust had landed on his head! He used to giggle to himself.

Come back Dad, please come home more, he always wished.
And one day his wish came true. Dad came home and in his arms was
a little puppy, he would grow up to be a Great Dane called Blue.

Charlie and Blue went everywhere together and suddenly life for Charlie was not so lonely. Somebody understood him when Blue would lift his leg to mark his territory on the side of Billy Barrow.
Charlie would laugh, he actually laughed for the first time in ages.

When Charlie arrived at school with Blue, one of his fathers' homeless friends would sit outside and mind Blue until Charlie came out, it was Charlie and Blue's way of sharing kindness. Charlie knew what it was like, to feel alone, he even donated his sandwich every day.

Mum could never understand why Charlie and Blue could eat so much every evening. And as soon as the dark arrived, boom they headed to their room.

What mum didn't know is that every night when it got dark
Charlie would see Larry the Lamp Post come alive and shine his light on
Charlie and the adventures would begin.

Blue would jump in Billy Barrow and Charlie rode Larry, and off out into the night skies they travelled to explore the stars and the interesting shapes his dad told him about but never had time to show him.

He watched in wonder as the constellations took shape before his eyes.

Each night he would discover a different shape to behold.

The Great Bear
bowed at him.

The Bird of Paradise
smiled at him.

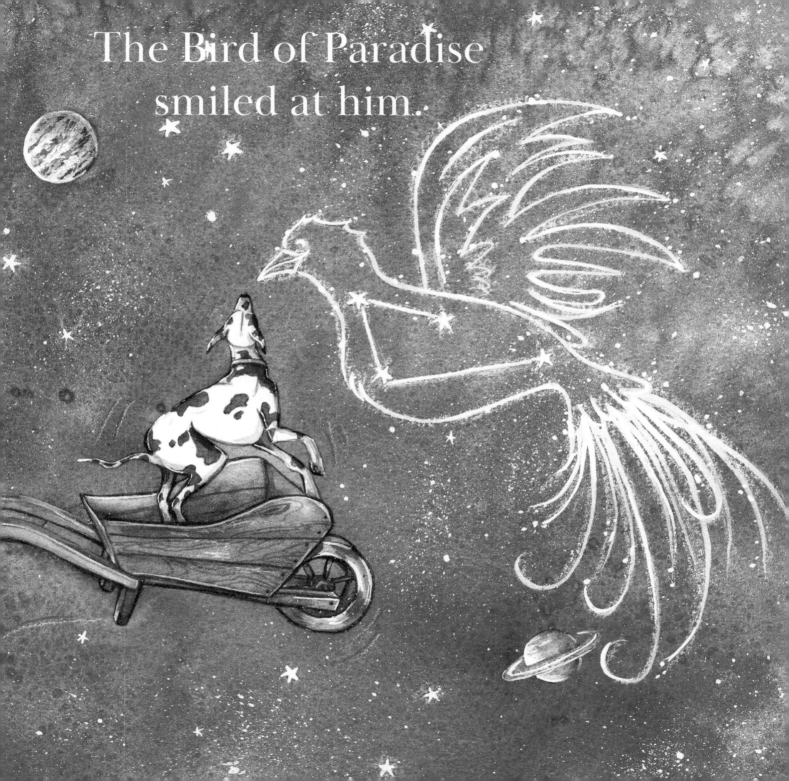

The Southern Cross
marked his journey.

The Giraffe
stood tall and strong

The Eagle
guided his way.

The Ram
was strong.

Charlie and his friends would gallop in and around each star in the constellation, weaving themselves through the night sky with a magical trail of light that beamed behind them from Larry the Lamp Post's magical glow.

It could be seen from far and wide and no one would know of the galactic adventures Charlie and his friends would have together.

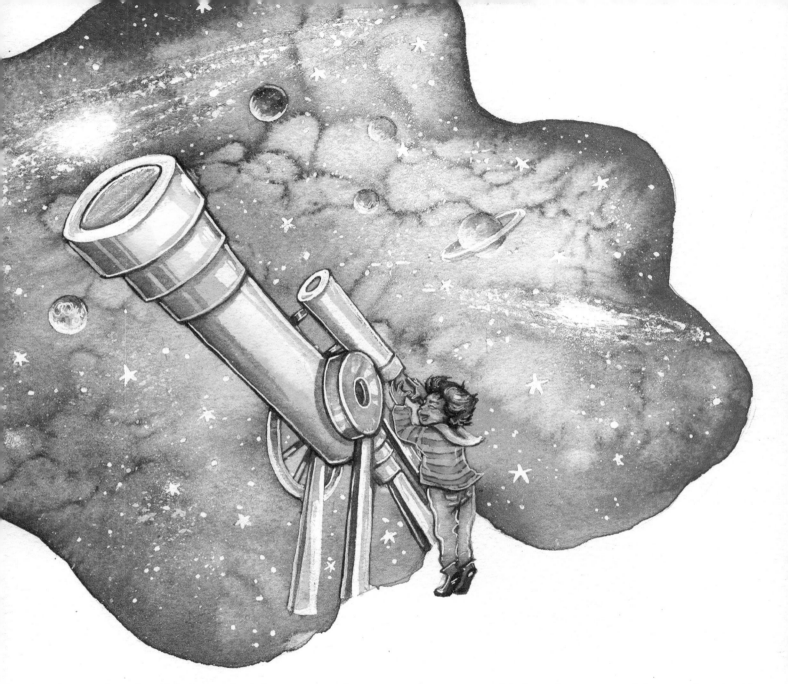

With each adventure Charlie gained so much strength that he was able to do well at school and even asked his dad if he could visit the observatory he worked at because he knew that he wanted to be an astronomer too.

Fun Constellation Facts

1. We have the Greek and Romans to thank for the names of the constellations with many of them relating to their mythological heroes and legends.

2. There are 88 officially recognized constellations by the International Astronomical Union (IAU).

3. 36 of the 88 constellations lie in the northern skies and the remaining 52 are visible in the southern skies.

4. It's not just stars that make up the constellations, many nebulae and galaxies are also included!

5. The constellations that are visible throughout the year depend on where you live on the Earth.

6. Constellations rise in the East and set in the West every night, but they also rise and set slightly earlier each day.

7. The sun passes through 13 constellations in a year, but astrologers only use 12, leaving out Ophiuchus the serpent bearer.

8. Hydra the water snake is the biggest of all constellations.

Space Facts

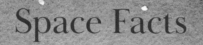

1. The word "astronaut" means "star sailor" in its origins.

2. Space is completely silent because there is no air in space, and air is needed to carry the sound vibrations.

3. Stars twinkle because of the way light is disrupted as it passes through Earth's atmosphere.

4. There are 9,096 stars visible to the naked eye in the entire sky.

5. There are more stars in space than there are grains of sand on the Earth.

6. The more massive a star, the shorter its lifespan

7. In China, the Milky Way is known as the "Silver River".

8. Only 5% of the universe is visible from Earth.

Constellation and Space Facts kindly contributed by
MATT WOODS
from Perth Observatory

PERTH

OBSERVATORY

For a bonus list of Planet Facts visit serenitypress.org

Star name: Sarah's Star

RA 15h 18m 24.72s -12° 55' 29.4'' dec

HD 135966

STAR ASTRONOMICAL COORDINATES

★ ID: HD 135966
  Constellation: Libra
  Right ascension: 15h18m24.72s
  Declination: -12°55'29.4"

FIND YOUR STAR HERE:

Sarah's Star Shines Bright

Kindness is a superpower

Sarah's Star is always watching, it shines rays of light,
it's superpower is called kindness.

If you look up to it, you will feel a blast of kindness that will stay with
you forever, whenever you need a bolt of goodness,
take a moment and look for Sarah's star.

You are never alone.

Sarah's star embodies the total value of kindness and goodness of Sarah,
and the stratospherically golden global heart.

When the sky is midnight blue look to the co-ordinates on the opposite page
and you will see Sarah's Star

Sarah x

SARAH,
DUCHESS OF YORK

Sarah's Trust

20% of all proceeds from the sales of **Duchess Serenity Press** books
goes directly to **Sarah's Trust.**

We are dedicated to being a voice and ambassador for the forgotten women,
children, families and communities around the world.
Sarah's Trust works with, and supports, organisations and
initiatives that reflect the ethos of our charitable work.

www.sarahstrust.com

More books from the *Duchess Serenity Press* Kindness Collection
picture books proudly raising funds for *Sarah's Trust.*

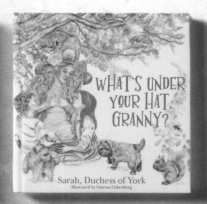

First published by Serenity Press (Serenity Press Kids) in 2021
www.serenitypress.org

National Library of Australia
Cataloguing in-Publication entry:
1. Juvenile fiction - general. 2. Juvenile fiction - adventure 3. Juvenile Fiction - Friendship

Sarah, Duchess of York (Sarah, Duchess of York), The Adventure of Charlie, Blue and Larry Lamp Post
ISBN: 978-0-6452689-0-4 (hc)
ISBN: 978-0-6451762-9-2 (e)

Editor: Teena Raffa-Mulligan
Cover, illustrations and text design © Emma Stuart

Lightning Source UK Ltd.
Milton Keynes UK
UKHW051108131221
395470UK00002B/29